For Nick and Matt.

H.E.

For my brother, who has taken care of
me since we were little and still does,
though from a distance.

A.L.

First American Edition 2020
Kane Miller, A Division of EDC Publishing
www.kanemiller.com
First published in Great Britain 2020 by Caterpillar Books Ltd,
an imprint of the Little Tiger Group
Text by Harriet Evans
Text copyright © Caterpillar Books Ltd 2020
Illustrations copyright © Andrés Landazábal 2020
All rights reserved
Library of Congress Control Number: 2019942865
Printed in China
ISBN: 978-1-68464-051-5
CPB/1400/1583/0720
10 9 8 7 6 5 4 3

A Celebration

of

Brothers

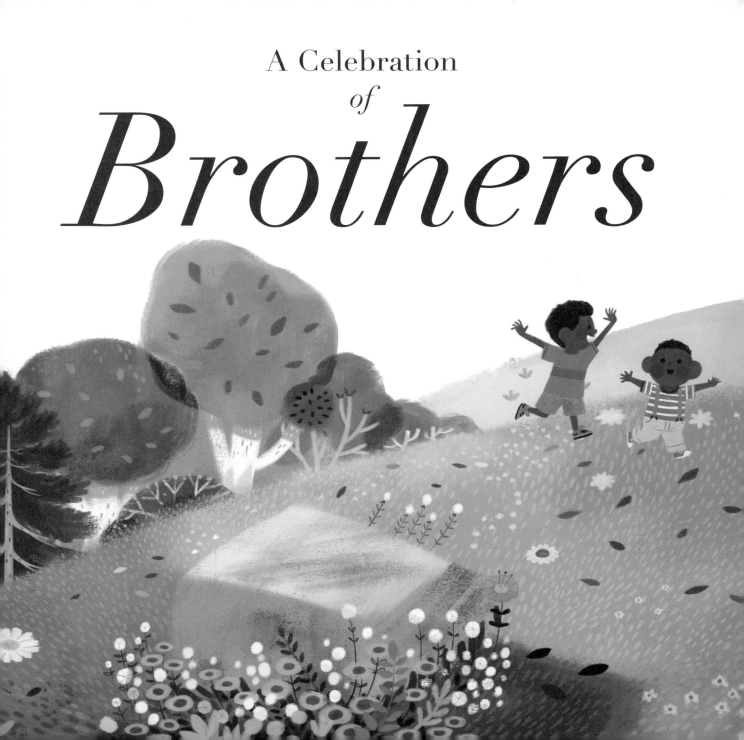

Families are different,
with brothers big and small.

Stepbrothers

or half brothers,

we love them, one and all.

They'll be there on
your worst days,

to help you dry your eyes.

They'll be there on your best days,
when your heart soars to the skies.

A brand-new baby brother,

to take under your wing,

is a rare and precious present,

an unsung song to sing.

You might find your brothers in the friends you make.

Sailing on adventures, your bond will never break.

Brothers can make life messy,

and upset the best-laid plans.

But they will remain beside you ...
a pair of helping hands.

Big brothers lift you up, they teach you all they know;

a playmate and a mentor, to help you as you grow.

Always wearing
hand-me-downs

can soon get tired and old.

But sharing has its upside,
like trust and secrets told.

Brothers might annoy you
and sometimes make you scream,

but when you work together,
you make the perfect team.

Brothers will support your dreams
and who you want to be.
Though you may be opposites,

he's
the sky ...

... to your deep sea.

Families are different,

with brothers big and small.

Stepbrothers or half brothers ...

... we love them ...

one and all.

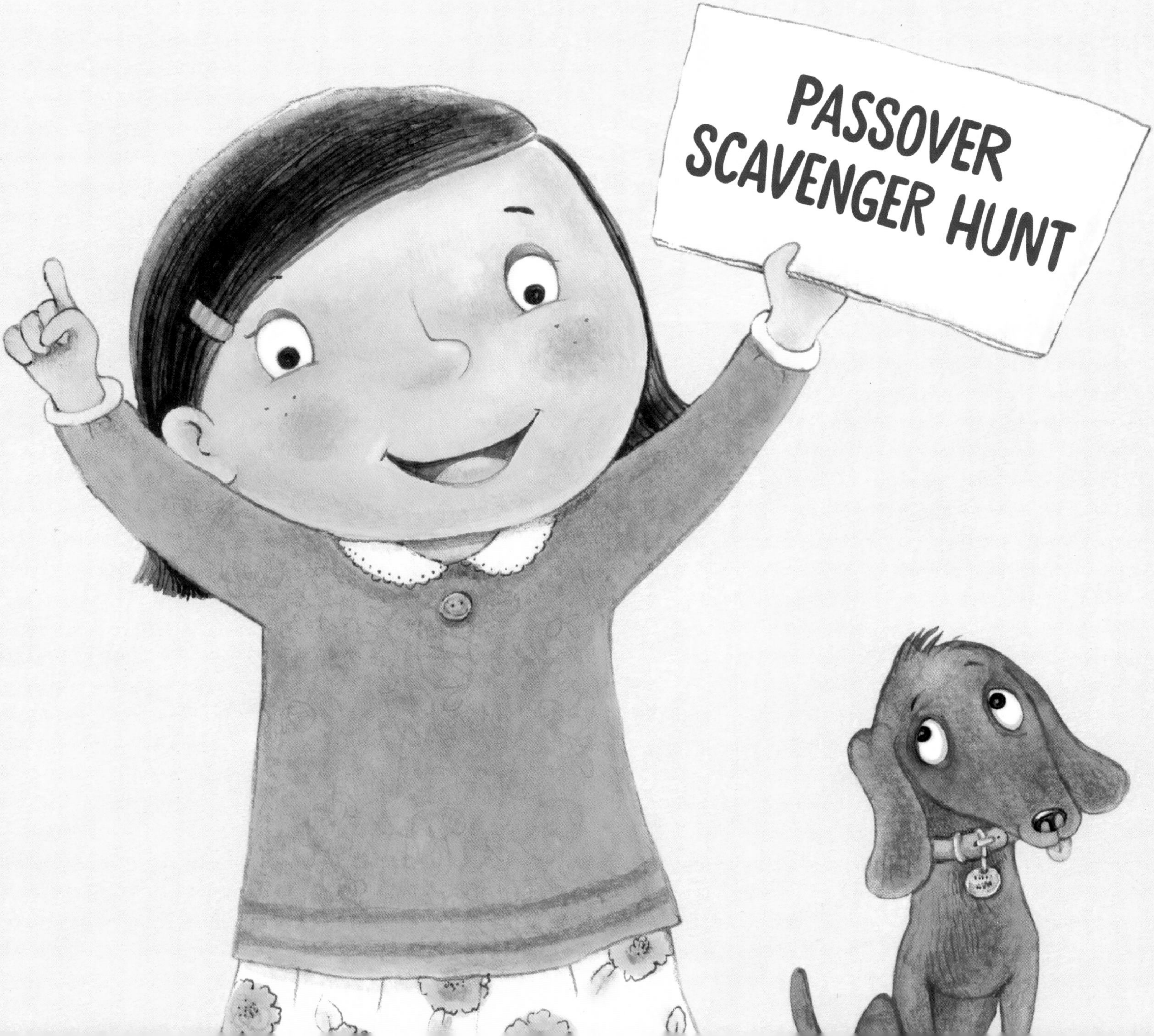
PASSOVER
SCAVENGER HUNT

For my four greatest loves: Steven, Brandon, Robert and Alex. Also for my grandfather, Robert Shapiro, whose epic seders inspired this book —S.S.

To my mom and dad who always believed in me —M.S.

ABOUT PASSOVER

Passover celebrates the exodus of the Israelite slaves from Egypt and the birth of the Jewish people as a nation. The spring holiday begins with a festive meal called a seder. Families gather to read the haggadah, a book that tells the story of the Jewish people's historic journey to freedom. Children are involved in asking questions about the rituals and in searching for a hidden matzah called the afikomen. During the holiday week no hametz (leavened food, such as bread) is eaten. Matzah takes the place of bread.

KAR-BEN PUBLISHING
A division of Lerner Publishing Group, Inc.
241 First Avenue North
Minneapolis, MN 55401 USA
1-800-4-KARBEN

Website address: www.karben.com

Main body text set in Bawdy 16/21. Typeface provided by Chank.

Library of Congress Cataloging-in-Publication Data

Names: Silva, Shanna, author. | Sakamoto, Miki, illustrator.
Title: Passover scavenger hunt / by Shanna Silva ; illustrated by Miki Sakamoto.
Description: Minneapolis, Minneapolis : Kar-Ben Publishing, [2016] | 2016 | Ages 4–9, K to grade 3.
Identifiers: LCCN 2016008977 (print) | LCCN 2016009595 (ebook) | ISBN 9781467789370 (lb : alk. paper) | ISBN 9781467794220 (pb : alk. paper) | ISBN 9781512427226 (eb pdf)
Subjects: | CYAC: Passover—Juvenile fiction.
Classification: LCC PZ7.S585644 Pas 2016 (print) | LCC PZ7.S585644 (ebook) | DDC [E]—dc23

LC record available at http://lccn.loc.gov/2016008977

Manufactured in the United States of America
1-38123-19967-3/2/2016

PASSOVER
SCAVENGER
HUNT

SHANNA SILVA

iLLUSTRATiONS BY MiKi SAKAMOTO

KAR-BEN
PUBLISHING

Rachel had a plan.

Every Passover, Great-Uncle Harry led the family seder and hid the afikomen.

But Great-Uncle Harry was a terrible hider. Rachel and her cousins knew all his hiding places:

in the tissue box,

on the bookshelf,

behind the goldfish bowl.

Rachel had an idea! It was a few hours before the seder, and Great-Uncle Harry was taking a nap with Rachel's puppy, Hotdog.

"Uncle Harry, you're so tired," said Rachel. "Why don't you let me hide the afikomen for you tonight so you can relax?"

Great-Uncle Harry smiled. "Good idea." And he went back to sleep.

Rachel grabbed her markers, scissors,
and a big piece of white cardboard.
She had a lot of work to do.

During the seder, Rachel squirmed with excitement. Great-Uncle Harry took the middle matzah and broke it in half. He wrapped it in a white napkin and passed it to Rachel.

"This year Rachel is hiding the afikomen," he announced.

Rachel held up an envelope labeled CLUE NUMBER ONE.

"We're doing an Afikomen Scavenger Hunt!" said Rachel. "I've hidden six envelopes around the house. Each envelope has a puzzle piece and a riddle that will lead you to the next clue. Once you find the clues and solve the puzzle, you'll find the afikomen!"

CLUE NUMBER ONE

She handed the envelope to Michael. Inside he found a cardboard puzzle piece and a riddle that he read aloud:

Karpas is parsley, fresh and green.
Find Clue Number Two
Where green is the scene.

"We have to look where green is the scene," said Jack.

Jack went into the living room. Climbing onto the sofa, he looked up at the painting on the wall. He reached behind the frame and found CLUE NUMBER TWO.

Michael pulled out the new riddle.

"Read it to us, Michael," said Jack.

The egg is for spring, when everything grows.
Find Clue Number Three
Where the bald man glows.

Michael and Jack stared at the clue, scratching their heads.

David smiled and tiptoed down to the basement.

There on the shelf stood Great-Uncle Harry's tennis trophy, which was shaped like a tennis player—a bald tennis player.

David pulled out CLUE NUMBER THREE and another puzzle piece.

"I found it!" yelled David. The others raced downstairs and David read the clue aloud.

The shankbone reminds us of when the Jews fled.
Find Clue Number Four
Where Frank rests his head.

"That doesn't make sense. Who is Frank?" asked Jack.

Rachel giggled. "You'll have to figure it out."

"Please give us a hint," David begged.

"Maybe Frank isn't a *who*, but a *what*," said Rachel.

Rachel's puppy thumped down the stairs, tail wagging, and drool flying.

"Hey, it's Hotdog!" Michael exclaimed. "Hotdog is another word for Frank!"

"I know where Hotdog rests his head!" Michael said. He pointed to the dog bed. Under the cushion was CLUE NUMBER FOUR.

Apple-y charoset reminds us of bricks.
Find Clue Number Five
Where Rachel does tricks.

"Rachel's magic set!" Jack shouted.

"Lead the way, Jack," Rachel said.

In Rachel's closet, behind the stuffed animals, underneath her pink boots, was her box of magic tricks—and CLUE NUMBER FIVE.

Maror is bitter. I don't like the taste!
Find Clue Number Six
Where we recycle—not waste.

The scavenger hunt team dashed to the kitchen, practically knocking over Mom and Aunt Sarah.

David reached under the recycling bin for CLUE NUMBER SIX and the last puzzle piece.

Mazel Tov, cousins! Use your sharp eyes
To assemble the puzzle
And find your big prize.

CLUE NUMBER SIX

Michael, David, and Jack spread
the puzzle pieces on the floor.

They moved the pieces around
until they fit together.

"It's a seder plate!" David said. "It has all the clues from our scavenger hunt: karpas, egg, shankbone, charoset, and maror."

"So where's the afikomen?" Michael asked.

"I know!" said Jack.

He raced to the dining room and lifted the seder plate from the table. Underneath was the afikomen wrapped in a white napkin!

"How did you get it under there, Rachel?" asked David. "You were with us the whole time!"

"Uncle Harry, did you see her sneak back?" said Jack.

"I didn't see a thing," said Great-Uncle Harry. He winked at Rachel. "I've just been sitting here resting. Right, Rachel?"

"Right, Uncle Harry," she answered.